© 2007 Smith, Bonappétit & Son, Montreal, Canada,
Badiâa Sekfali (text) and Jean-Marie Benoit (illustrations).

Legal Deposit: 1st quarter 2007
Bibliothèque et Archives nationales du Québec
Library and Archives Canada

The publisher wishes to acknowledge the support of the Canada Council for the Arts for this publishing program.
We are also thankful to the SODEC.

The translation of this book was made possible through the financial support of the Canada Council
for the Arts and Heritage Canada through the Book Publishing Industry Development Program.
Government of Quebec—Tax credit for book publishing— Administered by SODEC

ISBN: 978-1-897118-19-1

The Rooster Prince
was first published under the direction of Catherine Germain.
Graphic design: Mathilde Hébert
Arabic calligraphy: Amine Benzaïd
Editing, French edition: Sylvie Roche
Editing, English edition: Stuart Ross
Proofreading: Marie Lauzon

Distributor for Canada
Fraser Direct
100 Armstrong Avenue
Georgetown, ON L7G 5S4

Printed in Canada by Litho Milles-Îles ltée.

Library and Archives Canada Cataloguing in Publication

Sekfali, Badiâa, 1947-
[Farouj le coq. English]
The rooster prince / written by Badiâa Sekfali ; illustrated
by Jean-Marie Benoit ; translated by Jane Macaulay.

Translation of: Farouj le coq.
For ages 5-8.
ISBN 978-1-897118-19-1

I. Benoit, Jean-Marie, 1965- II. Macaulay, Jane III. Title.
IV. Title: Farouj le coq. English.

PS8637.E485F3713 2007   jC843'.6   C2006-905038-4

The Rooster Prince

فروج

AN ALGERIAN FOLKTALE
TEXT
BADIÂA SEKFALI
ILLUSTRATIONS
JEAN-MARIE BENOIT

TRANSLATION: JANE MACAULAY

*For Sidi, my father, who showed us the world through his stories,
in the shade of the grapevine.*

B.S.

Smith, Bonappétit & Son
Montreal, Toronto

حا نجيتك : هاو! هاو!... ما ينشا فش

Here it comes! It's here... but it's already gone! What is it?[1]

Once upon a time, in a faraway land, there lived a King and Queen who desperately wanted to have a child. They were very pious and very good to their subjects, but their happiness was marred by the lack of an heir. The King worried about who would someday succeed him as ruler of the kingdom.

One day, the King asked a wise man known as Cheikh-El-Moudaber to come to the palace. It was said that this sage could find an answer to any problem one might have. The King explained his difficulty and asked if there was some way of resolving it. He hoped that some magical prayer would persuade God to take pity on him and give him the child he so longed for. The wise man told him that the most likely reason his prayers had gone unanswered was that they hadn't reached God's ears. He explained that there was a whole army of djinns[2] who were jealous of the King's piety and generosity, and who took a malicious pleasure in diverting his prayers towards the special cupboards where unfulfilled prayers were collected. The wise man said that the best way for the King to fool these demons was to use the name of an animal to refer to the child he wanted so badly. The djinns would misread the prayer and let it go through. The King had only to pray harder than ever and God would understand what he was really asking for.

Following this advice, the King made a new prayer. Hoping to touch God's heart but keep his true intentions hidden from the djinns, the King asked for a little chick as his heir. And God granted the King his wish.

⚘ 4 ⚘

A few months later, the Queen gave birth to a downy, golden baby chick – a little bird whose sweet chirping filled the palace with joy. The King, disappointed that God had followed his wish to the letter rather than understanding his intention, took this turn of events in his stride and declared that the kingdom at last had an heir. But knowing that it was ridiculous to have a chick as a crown prince, he lodged the newborn bird in an isolated wing of the palace and assigned a special nursemaid to feed him the finest grain in the kingdom. But the chick would have none of this and accepted only the best milk. He grew very quickly on this diet and soon became a true *farouj*[3] – a real little rooster.

His feathers became ever brighter and more beautiful, and his ivory beak grew ever finer and sharper. He bore his delicately sculpted red cockscomb proudly on his head, like a crown. The long feathers of his wings were so agile that he could use them like fingers and play games of skill just like the humans with whom he lived. His feet were covered with pearly scales right down to his exquisite claws, which were regularly filed, pumiced and polished by handmaids assigned exclusively to this task. Farouj was clearly an exceptionally beautiful bird. And – even more remarkably – surrounded by the servants and caretakers that the King considered appropriate for a royal son, Farouj developed the ability to speak.

The years passed and Farouj reached the age of reason, and wished to marry. He expressed this wish to his father, who, after the initial shock had passed, had his servants bring the loveliest pullets in the kingdom, so that his son might choose the one he liked best. But the young rooster did not even glance at them and explained to his father that he wanted a real young woman as his bride.

Unable to refuse his heir anything, but nonetheless sceptical about his chances of success, the King sent messengers throughout the land to seek some unfortunate maiden who would be willing to marry a young rooster. Aware that this quest was quite preposterous, he promised that the family of such a young woman would thenceforth live a tranquil life, with every need provided for. He hoped that with this promise, some poor father, struggling to keep his family fed, might offer one of his daughters in exchange for a future free of cares.

Soon afterwards, a young woman presented herself at the palace. Her parents, enticed by the King's offer, had persuaded her to accept by telling her that she should take all the gifts she would be given and then wring the young rooster's neck on her wedding night. That way she would be rid of a very unusual husband and have enough riches for a dowry that would practically guarantee her a more fortunate marriage later on. The young woman had jumped for joy at the prospect and accepted her parents' proposal. After all, the husband on offer was simply a fowl, just like the birds whose throats were slit for feasts. Thus soothing her conscience, she went merrily to the ceremony that would make her rich for the rest of her days.

A great feast took place and the King covered the young woman in gold and precious stones. Then he invited her to go to the wedding chamber where her rooster husband awaited her. When night fell and the servants withdrew from the room, the bird suddenly transformed into a splendid young man, his eyes blazing with rage. "And so," he cried, "you thought you would wring my neck, as if I were a common fowl! Well then, you have chosen your own death!" And with these words, he sprang upon her and wrung her neck. The young woman fell down dead and Farouj, satisfied, went to bed and slept the sound sleep of the just.

For this proud rooster was not like others of his kind. Before his birth, when the King had reworded his prayer so that it might be granted, the djinns had discovered his ruse and cast a spell on the royal baby. He would be a rooster by day and a human by night throughout his entire life. But a malek[4] who happened to be passing by had softened the evil spell – if in time the young rooster managed to show his sterling nature by overcoming a series of ordeals and thus win the true love of a young bride, he would be freed from the charm and keep his human form. If, on the other hand, he was unable to awaken such feelings, he would remain a rooster forever. This is why the unusual chick refused to act like an ordinary bird. He had to nourish the young man dormant within him, obtaining the finest foods and acquiring the noblest principles.

The next day, when the handmaids discovered the lifeless body of the young woman, they realized that their master was not just an ordinary rooster and that a djinn must be hiding inside him. They were seized with terror and went at once to the King to say that they would no longer serve such a strange prince. The King understood their fear, but asked them not to say a word to anyone, for he still hoped to find a young woman who would make his son happy. So he arranged for new handmaids to serve the Prince. When his son repeated his wish to marry, the King once again sent messengers to the four corners of the land to seek a maiden who was willing to unite her destiny with that of a creature so unusual, but also so rich.

Now, in an isolated corner of a faraway mountain, there lived a poor family that barely had enough to eat, even though the father worked himself to the bone. The children did their best to help. They gathered branches and made them into bundles of kindling, or picked wild berries and fruit that they arranged prettily in little woven baskets lined with fig leaves. Then the older children would take the bundles and the little baskets to neighbouring villages, where they sold them or traded them for anything that might help to feed their younger brothers and sisters. They all loved each other and did for each other what they could. So when the eldest daughter heard of the King's offer, she decided to accept. After all, it seemed like a fair exchange. She would give the King's presents of money and jewels to her family and live with this prince that people told such strange stories about. And even if he turned out to be an ogre, she didn't care − she would give up life itself if it meant better days for her family.

So the girl presented herself at the palace and said that she was ready to accept the royal offer. A grand ceremony was prepared, and the bride-to-be − who had known only the cold water of the mountain wadi[5] − was given a luxurious steam bath. In the soothing warmth of the bath, she was massaged, washed and perfumed by handmaids in preparation for the wedding. She accepted all this attention serenely, thinking it might be her last pleasure before being eaten alive by the strange creature she was to wed. The maids then dressed her in the finest robes in the kingdom and fitted her with a truly regal headdress. Thus arrayed, her beauty shone, and all who saw her were secretly filled with sadness at the thought that such a lovely young woman was about to lose her life. They led her sorrowfully to the wedding chamber, convinced they would never see her alive again.

Alone in the chamber, the young woman awaited her royal husband. She was quite astonished when she saw a beautiful rooster enter the room. She took him onto her lap and stroked his crest, speaking softly to him: "Oh beautiful Farouj, the mere sight of your beauty comforts me in the face of the death I will no doubt meet when your master arrives!"

At that moment, the miracle happened – a mantle of feathers fell from the young rooster and in its place stood a magnificent prince. The young woman was speechless with wonder and thanked God for the wonderful fate he had in store for her.

Young Prince Farouj, finding his new wife full of virtues, told her his story and made her promise not to divulge his secret to anyone. She agreed, but eventually she could no longer withstand all the questions her family asked, as they wondered how she could bear to live with such a strange being. So she confided in her mother how her pretty little rooster by day became a handsome prince by night, when his feather mantle fell, and how the situation suited her quite perfectly.

One day, the mother, who like every mother wanted only the best for her daughter, decided that her eldest should live the life of a true queen, by day as well as by night. She bribed a palace servant, promising her a purse filled with gold coins if she managed to throw the Prince's feather mantle into the fire after he removed it at bedtime. In the middle of the night, the maid tiptoed into the royal couple's bedroom, snatched up the feather mantle and threw it onto the glowing embers in the fireplace. Having done this wicked deed, she ran to get her reward as fast as her legs could carry her, for she knew full well that, after what she had done, she would no longer be welcome at the palace.

The acrid smell of burning feathers roused the couple. Leaping from the bed, Prince Farouj dashed to the fireplace. He pulled the mantle out and, charred as it was, threw it over his shoulders. Flying out the window, he had time only to shout to the princess, "If you want to find me, I will be at Djebel Ouaq Ouaq!" The young woman burst into tears, realizing that she had lost her beloved Prince because she had betrayed his secret. When the King and Queen rushed into the room, she told them what had happened and said, "I am leaving to search for my dear husband, and until I have found him, I shall not return!"

She filled a goatskin container with leben[6], packed a bag of wheat cakes, took a few of her finest pieces of jewellery and left the palace at dawn. She walked for a long, long time, asking everyone she met if they could tell her how to get to Djebel Ouaq Ouaq.[7] They invariably replied, making vague hand gestures, "It's very far away, in that direction..."

Eventually, reaching a little village, she asked to see the Cheikh-El-Moudaber of the region. The villagers pointed to a tumbledown house, sitting alone on a mountaintop. She made her way up to the house, and there she found a little old man, all dressed in white, lost in thought. "Tell me, Holy Man," she asked, "what must I do to find the way to Djebel Ouaq Ouaq? I have been walking for many days without stopping, but nobody will tell me the way. Who should I ask and what should I do?"

The old man was silent for a while before he answered. "What trials await you, my child, before you reach this djebel, whose very name fills people with fear! You must first go eastward until you meet the ogress who guards the road leading to Djebel Ouaq Ouaq. You'll see, she is huge and extremely dangerous, but you'll have a good chance of succeeding if you follow my advice carefully. Every day, around noon, the ogress goes and sits in the middle of the road to grind her wheat into flour. Since her breasts are enormous, she tosses one behind her back, so it doesn't get in her way as she turns her big millstone. Find a way to touch this breast. When she turns around to gobble you up, offer her your goatskin of leben to drink, and while she's drinking, touch her other breast. If you manage to do this, she can be of great assistance to you. That is all I can tell you, and may Allah be with you, my poor child!" The brave young woman took up her bag of supplies and set off in the direction the old wise man had indicated.

After walking for a long time, she at last glimpsed the ogress, sitting in the middle of the rocky road and singing at the top of her lungs. The young woman crept up on tiptoe and, with a rapid movement, brushed her fingertips against the breast flung over the ogress's back. The ogress let out a great roar and wheeled around, ready to gobble up the fool who had dared to disturb her like this. The young woman deftly held out her goatskin and touched the other breast – and then took two big steps backward, out of the reach of this man-eating creature. But now the ogress had become suddenly calm and said to her, "One of my breasts belongs to Aissa,[8] and the other to Moussa.[9] If you'd touched only one and not both of my reserves of eternal nourishment, I would have swallowed your blood in one gulp and devoured your flesh with one bite, and your bones would have cracked like thunder in the sky! But you knew how to quell my temper, so now ask me for whatever you want."

The young woman told the ogress her story and begged her to point the way to Djebel Ouaq Ouaq. The ogress removed three hairs from her head and gave them to her, saying, "Continue along the road in this direction until you pass the blue mountain you can see on the horizon. From there, follow the flight of a great blue raven. It will lead you to its dwelling place on the highest tower of the castle of Djebel Ouaq Ouaq, where your husband is imprisoned. At the foot of the castle, burn one of my hairs. Its smoke will point the way to his room. Knock at the door and it will be opened by the woman who keeps him prisoner. She is very greedy, so offer her one of your jewels and then maybe she'll agree to help you."

The young woman thanked the ogress and, without waiting a minute longer, continued her long journey to find the Prince who she so longed to see again. Her fatigue had disappeared and the prospect of seeing her dear husband once more lent wings to her feet.

After passing the blue mountain, she caught sight of a beautiful blue-black raven. She hid behind a large rock and waited for twilight, when the bird usually returned home. She followed its flight, going as fast as she could, even though she had to make her way through sharp branches and stinging nettles. But nothing, absolutely nothing, could divert her from her goal, neither hunger nor her ever-growing pain. Finally, she reached an immense castle with lofty towers that held many ravens' nests. The great blue raven settled down for the night and the young woman could at last catch her breath. Now she had to find a way through the great castle's doorless walls.

Following the ogress's advice, she burned one of the three hairs she had been given. As if by magic, a doorway appeared. She entered it and found herself in a long corridor that led to a vast hall that had but one other door. She knocked on the door, her heart in her mouth.

The jailer flung open the door, shouting, "Who dares to disturb my dear husband and me?" The young woman opened her bag and took out one of the magnificent pieces of jewellery she had brought with her. She offered it to the jailer in exchange for a few minutes with the prisoner. The jailer, whose greedy eyes had spied the rest of the jewellery, at once thought up a plan for getting her hands on it all. She asked the young woman to come back a little later. Then she prepared the Prince's supper, adding a few drops of a magic potion that caused him to fall into a deep sleep. She then invited her visitor to enter the Prince's chamber. The young woman shook the prisoner, begged him to speak to her and finally pummelled him with her fists – but to no avail. He continued to sleep like a log. Realizing it was hopeless, she called the jailer, who let her out by another door leading directly outside the castle. There, the young woman rested while she thought long and hard about how best to rescue her husband, who she had been unable to awake.

The next morning, the Prince awoke aching all over and saw that his body was covered with bruises. He went to the window to examine himself in better light and said to himself out loud, "What on earth happened last night? Why do I feel so awful?" A raven flying past the window answered, "Last night a beautiful young woman with love in her eyes tried to take you away, but she found you sound asleep! Ouaq! Ouaq! Too bad for he who sleeps!" Intrigued, the Prince pondered what the bird had said, while absent-mindedly offering leftover bits of his supper to a young raven that had alighted on the windowsill. At once, the raven fell into a deep sleep. The young man realized at once that this food was the cause of his discomfort and he decided not to eat anything that his jailer gave him. So he wouldn't die of hunger, he asked a third raven to bring him some berries in its beak. When evening fell, he went to bed but he resolved to stay awake, on the alert for anything unusual that might happen.

During this time, the dauntless young woman had been thinking about the best way to reunite with her beloved. For there was no question of leaving without him after she had come so far and suffered so much. She made another tour of the walls and, again finding no opening, decided to burn another of the precious hairs the ogress had given her. The smoke rose into the air and formed a giant finger pointing to a precise spot in the wall. She walked up to it and, as before, a doorway opened onto a long corridor. The young woman slipped inside, filled with hope that she and her beloved would soon be on their way. Knocking at the door at the far end of the corridor, she was greeted by the jailer, who grinned craftily at the thought of soon being decked out in all her visitor's jewels. The jailer picked out the most beautiful piece of the remaining jewellery and asked the young woman to wait a bit while she prepared her husband, as she called the Prince, for his visitor. Then she went to prepare a meal with the magic potion and gave it to the Prince. He pretended to take a bite of his supper and immediately feigned deep sleep.

A few minutes later, the young woman entered his room. Seeing him asleep again, she rushed to him crying, "Wake up, my love! I've suffered so much to find you and I will never leave you alone again. If you won't awake, I'll stay here with you, even if it means I have to kill the jailer!" Hearing these words, Farouj recognized the voice of his dear wife and opened his eyes at once. They fell into each other's arms and related everything that had happened to them since that unhappy day when the young wife had so unwisely confided the rooster's secret to her family. Prince Farouj told her that by enduring such trials, she had delivered him forever from the spell that had burdened him until now.

Overjoyed to be reunited and realizing that their ordeals had only deepened their love, they resolved to leave, but the walls surrounding them revealed no opening. The young woman remembered that she still had the last hair from the ogress's head. She burned it, hoping it would show her a way out of the castle. The smoke stretched towards one of the walls, where a narrow passage suddenly opened, and the couple fled through it. Once outside, they set off for the royal palace – the young woman's heart growing lighter with every step, and Prince Farouj hopping and fluttering with happiness around her, for he had decided to keep his feather mantle until he was reunited with his parents.

When they arrived at the palace, a crowd welcomed them with ringing ululations,[10] even though the crown prince was in their eyes still just a young rooster.

Seeing such acclaim from his future subjects, Farouj could not resist the urge to show his true nature. With a shake, he let his feather mantle drop and stood before the crowd as a splendid young man, glowing with health and vitality.

The royal marriage was celebrated anew, and, just as the King and Queen had hoped, the young couple eventually blessed the palace with many children.

1 Tales from the Setifian High Plains, in Algeria, always begins with a little riddle. **The answer to this riddle: lightning**.

2 **Djinns** are evil spirits found in the Muslim tradition.

3 **Farouj** means rooster in Arabic.

4 **Malek** is the Arabic name for good spirits or "angels" in the Muslim tradition.

5 In Northern Africa, a **wadi** is a seasonal river that dries up in summer.

6 **Leben** is whey, or buttermilk, which is the liquid left after milk has been churned into butter.

7 **Djebel** is the Arabic word for mountain, and "**ouaq-ouaq**" represents the raucous cry of ravens.

8 **Aissa** is the name for Jesus in Arabic.

9 **Moussa** is the name for Moses in Arabic.

10 **Ululations** are high-pitched rhythmic cries traditionally made by women throughout the Arab world to express great emotion.

11 This expression is used by Algerian storytellers to announce the end of a tale.

هذا ما قلنى   هذا ما سمعنى

All that we have heard, we have now told you![11]